Dragon Owner's Manual
(by Sir Bertram the B...

Written by Catherine Baker

Illustrated by Carl Morris

Collins

Welcome, dragon owners!

Your new pet dragon
may seem big and
frightening, but just
follow my rules.

Sir Bertram the Bold

Bertie

How your dragon works

Learn how dragons make flames!

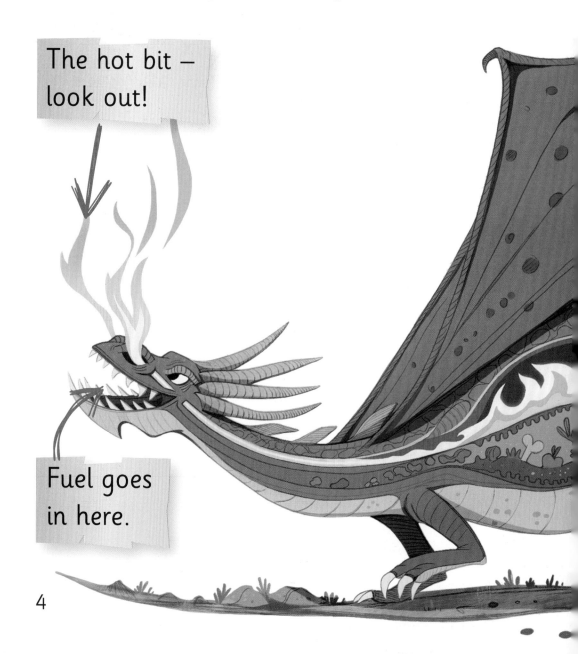

The hot bit –
look out!

Fuel goes
in here.

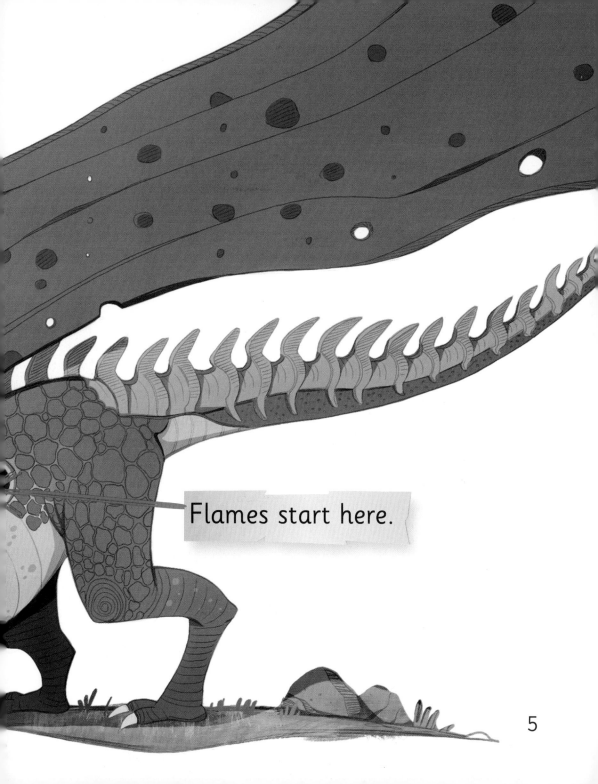

Flames start here.

A home for your dragon

First, check you have
room for a dragon.

Your dragon is quite big. He will not fit under your bed.

Dragons need their sleep!

Your dragon needs a heap of gold to sleep on.

If you don't have much gold, borrow some from a friend. (Always ask first!)

Dragon fuel

Dragons eat a lot!

Breakfast: a hundred toasted teacakes

Lunch: loads of turnip stew

Snack: beanburgers

Tea: pasta (lots)

Dinner: buckets of soup

11

Keeping clean

Get a broom with a long stick to clean your dragon. Don't stand too near!

My Bertie is always neat and fresh!

Keeping well

Your dragon must not get a cold — or its flames may go out!

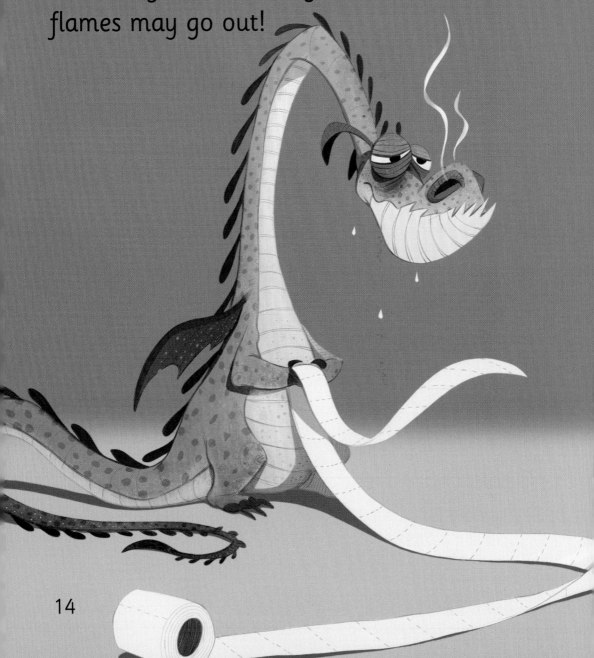

I made Bertie this fantastic scarf and hat.

Keeping fit

Your dragon must go on quests to keep fit.

Keep it away from damsels in distress!

damsel

Dragons at work!

Make your dragon work for you!
It can go shopping.

It can get rid of pests.

It can also heat your home.

Dragon fun and games

Dragons enjoy games! My Bertie likes playing leapfrog.

Find out what your dragon likes best!

chess

snap

hide and seek

21

What do dragons need?

Letters and Sounds: Phase 5

Word count: 243

Focus phonemes: /igh/ i, i-e /ai/ ay, a-e /oa/ o, oe, ow, o-e /oo/ ue, ew, ou, u-e /ee/ ie, ea /oi/ oy /ow/ ou /or/ our, al /er/ ir, or, ear /ear/ ere /e/ ea /u/ o-e

Common exception words: my, the, he, of, have, their, friend, to, what, do, be

Curriculum links: History

National Curriculum learning objectives: Reading/word reading: apply phonic knowledge and skills as the route to decode words; read accurately by blending sounds in unfamiliar words containing GPCs that have been taught; read common exception words; read other words of more than one syllable that contain taught GPCs; read aloud accurately books that are consistent with their developing phonic knowledge; re-read books to build up their fluency and confidence in word reading; Reading/comprehension: link what they have read or hear read to their own experiences; discuss word meanings; discuss the significance of the title and events

Developing fluency

- Take turns to read a page each with your child, discussing and practising the voice Sir Bertram might have.

Phonic practice

- Identify the words that have the /igh/ sound in and discuss how differently the same sound can be written. (*light, find, knight, kite*)
- Now ask your child to find words in the book that use the /ai/ sound.

Extending vocabulary

- The word **frightening** is used to describe a pet dragon. What other words could be used? (e.g. *scary, terrifying, petrifying, alarming*)
- What words would you use to describe Sir Bertram the Bold? (e.g. *silly, funny, amusing, unwise*)

Comprehension

- Turn to pages 22 and 23 and discuss the different elements that the manual says dragons need.
- Ask your child:
  - Can you describe Bertie the dragon? (e.g. *sharp teeth, red with large purple spots, huge, magnificent, fire-breathing, purple spikes*)